Picture-Perfect Tommy

Based on the TV series *Rugrats*® created by Arlene Klasky, Gabor Csupo, and
Paul Germain as seen on Nickelodeon®

SIMON SPOTLIGHT
An imprint of Simon & Schuster Children's Publishing Division
1230 Avenue of the Americas
New York, New York 10020

Manufactured in the United States of America
First Edition   2 4 6 8 10 9 7 5 3 1

Library of Congress Cataloging-in-Publication Data
Willson, Sarah.
Picture-perfect Tommy / by Sarah Willson.—1st ed.
p. cm. - (Ready-to-read ; #11)
"Based on the TV series Rugrats"-T.p. verso.
Summary: When Tommy and the other Rugrats go to the museum, one of
Tommy's paintings ends up on display.
ISBN 0-689-83596-5
[1. Babies—Fiction. 2. Painting—Fiction. 3. Museums—Fiction.] I. Rugrats
(Television program) II. Title. III. Series.
PZ7.W6845 Pi 2001
[E]-dc21
00-041947

Picture-Perfect
TOMMY

by Sarah Willson

illustrated by Robert Roper

Ready-to-Read

Simon Spotlight/Nickelodeon

New York   London   Toronto   Sydney   Singapore

"The kids love to paint," said Didi.
"Let's go to the Fine Art Museum."

"Sounds great," Betty said.

"Aw, Deed," cried Stu.
"There's a great ball game on TV!"

Didi gave Stu a look.

Stu sighed. "Okay. I'll tell Chas
and Howard we're leaving."

Didi picked up Dil.
She put him into his stroller.
Dil picked up Tommy's painting.
He put it into his stroller.

At the museum, Stu looked at a painting. "You call this *fine* art?" he said. "Please. This looks like something Tommy would do."

"Oh, Stu," said Didi, shaking her head.

Dil pulled out Tommy's picture and dropped it on the floor.

NOSE
ART TEEST

9

"Look!" said Didi. "There's the gift shop!"

"Look!" said Stu. "There's the ball game!
You go ahead," he said to Didi and
Betty. "We'll watch the kids."

The fathers watched the game.
The babies crawled away.

A guard picked up Tommy's picture.

He looked at it.
He looked at the painting on the wall.
Then the guard hurried away.

"What is this place called, Tommy?" asked Chuckie.

"It's called the Find Art You-See-'Um," Tommy replied. "I think people find art here. And you-see-'um on the walls!"

BALLERINA
ITSA FLOP

SOGGY FIVE
WILD FRED

The babies crawled past the guard.
He was showing something
to another grown-up.
"It must have been hidden
behind a painting!" said the other man.
"We must put it up right away!"

EYE-FULL
SID SCHLEP

THE YA\
Z. ZAZZZ

"I like this one," said Tommy.
"I wonder if the baby who made it
got in trouble for cutting up the newspaper."

"Is he on the potty?" asked Chuckie.
"I think so," said Tommy.

19

"That baby must have used up a lot of markers doing all those dots," said Phil.

DOTS DA BEACH
ED STIRPOT

"This baby didn't even have to clean up his spilled paint," said Lil.

MESSY
CANVAS

JACKIE
PULLOCK

"That baby had trouble staying inside the lines," said Kimi.

SELF PORTRAIT
MARK BOFFO

"This baby didn't know what to draw,"
said Chuckie.

23

"Look!" said Phil. "That baby got to draw on the wall!"

Just then Stu and Chas and Howard
dashed around a corner.

"Weeee!" said Dil.

"There you are!" said Stu.

"We thought we'd lost you guys,"
said Chas.

"Let's go find your mom," Stu said
to Tommy.

Dil pointed at a painting.
"Tomby!" he said excitedly.

"Hey, Tommy, isn't that your painting?"
Chuckie whispered.

"Yeah," said Tommy. "I guess they
finded my art. They must have wanted it
for the you-see-'um!"

UNTITLED

B. GOODY

THIS GREAT WORK OF ART HAS JUST BEEN FOUND. IT IS PROBABLY FROM THE ARTIST'S EARLY DAYS. SEE HOW THE BLUE PAINT HAS BEEN CAREFULLY MIXED. RED AND YELLOW HAVE BEEN USED FOR DRAMATIC EFFECT.

THE MUSEUM STAFF

"Look," said Didi, coming out of
the gift shop. "The kids like that painting!"
"I like it too," Stu said.
"But I still don't get this modern art.
Even Tommy could have done
a better job than some of these."

OOPS!
MEL DRIPPO

Stu chuckled. "Keep painting, sport. Maybe someday you'll have something hanging in here!"

ITLED

OODY

GREAT WORK
HAS JUST
UND. IT IS
BLY FROM
IST'S EARLY
EE HOW THE
NT HAS BEEN
Y MIXED. RED
LLOW HAVE
USED FOR
IC EFFECT.

SEUM STAFF